# MARVEL
## AFTER-SCHOOL
# HEROES
### GHOST-SPIDER'S UNBREAKABLE MISSION

By MacKenzie Cadenhead
Illustrated by Dave Bardin

SIMON SPOTLIGHT
NEW YORK LONDON TORONTO SYDNEY NEW DELHI

SIMON SPOTLIGHT
An imprint of Simon & Schuster Children's Publishing Division
1230 Avenue of the Americas, New York, New York 10020
This Simon Spotlight hardcover edition November 2024
All rights reserved, including the right of reproduction in whole or in part in any form.
SIMON SPOTLIGHT and colophon are registered trademarks of Simon & Schuster, LLC.
Simon & Schuster: Celebrating 100 Years of Publishing in 2024.
Also available in a Simon Spotlight paperback edition.
For information about special discounts for bulk purchases, please contact Simon & Schuster Special Sales at 1-866-506-1949 or business@simonadnschuster.com.
Text by Mackenzie Cadenhead
Illustrations by Dave Bardin
Cityscape illustration by Bakal/iStock
Designed by Nicholas Sciacca
Manufactured in the United States of America 1024 LAK
10 9 8 7 6 5 4 3 2 1
ISBN 978-1-6659-5909-4 (hc)
ISBN 978-1-6659-5908-7 (pbk)
ISBN 978-1-6659-5910-0 (ebook)

# CONTENTS

# Chapter 1:

# GREAT EGGSPECTATIONS

Gwen Stacy stared at the egg on her desk. Every student in Mr. Anzelone's science class had one. But what did her teacher want them to do with it? Gwen raised her hand.

"Thanks for the present, Mr. A," she said. "But next time how about a gift card?"

Mr. Anzelone laughed. "Sorry, Gwen. This is your homework. Over the weekend each of you will take special care of your egg. You can talk to it, take it on walks—"

"Watch a movie with it?" joked Gwen's classmate Amir.

"Whatever you want," Mr. Anzelone replied. "But remember, eggs are fragile. They can easily break. Your assignment is to bring the egg back on Monday in one piece. Show me how responsible you can be by caring for something so delicate."

The bell rang. "Your eggs are depending on you!" Mr. Anzelone said. "Class dismissed."

Gwen packed up her backpack. She spoke to her egg. "Don't worry about a thing, little eggy," she said, "because you hit the babysitting jackpot. I'm probably the most responsible kid in this class."

Gwen looked over at Amir, who was juggling his egg. "Scratch that," she said.

"I am *definitely* the most responsible kid in this class. But it's not just because I know not to toss you in the air." Gwen gently placed the egg in the folds of her white, black, and pink suit that she kept stored in one of the zippered pockets of her backpack. She leaned in and whispered, "It's because I'm a super hero."

The egg was speechless.

"It's true," Gwen continued in a hushed voice. "I'm your friendly neighborhood Ghost-Spider. I fight bad guys without breaking a sweat. So taking care of you will be a piece of cake."

Gwen looked at her watch. "Speaking of cake, there's a bakery near my drum lesson. That's where we're going now. If we hurry, we'll have

time to get a piece." Gwen flung her backpack over her shoulder . . .

And the egg flew out!

Gwen's hand shot out in a flash. She caught the little egg moments before it hit the floor.

"Oops," she said. She placed her egg back inside her backpack. "Guess I'd better zip this up, huh?" She gave a nervous giggle. "I mean, there's nothing to worry about, right? Super hero reflexes save the day!"

The egg did not reply.

With her backpack closed and firmly situated on one shoulder, Gwen set off for her drum lesson at the Stark Center. Gwen regularly attended drum lessons at the Stark Center several days a week after school. But today the idea of cake was still on her mind, so she took a shortcut to head toward the bakery first.

Turning down a side street, she walked past an abandoned warehouse. Gwen heard a strange commotion coming from inside.

"I thought 'abandoned' meant no one was supposed to be in it," she mumbled to herself. "Looks like something Ghost-Spider should go check out."

Gwen ducked into an alleyway and unzipped her backpack. "Listen, egg," she whispered as she changed into her super hero suit. "You stay here and I'll be back in a minute."

But as Ghost-Spider crept into the warehouse, she realized this job might take a little more than a minute. Standing before her was THE VULTURE!

# Chapter 2:

# *FOWL PLAY*

"Squawk!" A beak poked out from behind the bars of a large crate. Two henchmen were trying to lift the crate, but the bird's frantic movement was making it hard.

"Quiet that bird!" the Vulture snapped.

"But, boss," said the taller henchman, "it keeps peckin' at us through the bars!"

"Yeah," agreed the shorter one. "And it really hurts."

The Vulture glared at them. "Oh, it hurts, does it? Do you know what will hurt even more? The temper tantrum I'll throw if we don't get this crate into that van! We must sell this bird to the highest bidder, tonight!"

The Vulture glided over to the crate. The petrified bird cowered inside. "That's right. You are one of the rarest birds in the world. Many people would pay big bucks to own you. But do you know what's worth even more money? That priceless blue-spotted egg you're sitting on. So quit your yapping, or I'll take your egg and you'll get stuffed!"

"Shouldn't you, of all bad guys, be nicer to our feathered friends?" Ghost-Spider asked from the rafters. She flipped down onto the ground and landed in a crouch. Ghost-Spider spun a web onto the crate's door. She yanked. The crate burst open

and the rare bird quickly flew out!

"Get the egg!" the Vulture yelled to his minions. "I'll squash the spider."

The Vulture lunged at Ghost-Spider. She leapt just out of reach. She spun a web around a beam and pulled herself into the air.

"You're feisty today, birdbrain!" Ghost-Spider said. "Guess you really want that egg!" She swung around the abandoned warehouse. The Vulture flew after her.

"Stay still!" the criminal cried.

"I don't think that's how chases work," Ghost-Spider replied. "But, you know, we can just wing it."

"Graaah!" The Vulture flapped his wings furiously. Ghost-Spider could feel him closing in. Before he could catch her, she saw a narrow shaft that led to the ground, away from the Vulture. His mighty wings were too big to fit inside it, but it was the perfect size for a fast-thinking girl in a spider-suit. Ghost-Spider dove into the shaft. She heard the Vulture holler from above.

"Oof," she said as she hit the ground.

"Aw, man," said the tall henchman.
Ghost-Spider had landed right in front
of the pair. They were loading the blue-
spotted egg into the getaway van. One
of them charged at Ghost-Spider.
She rolled out of the way.

*Thwip!*

She webbed the henchman to the side
of the van. Then she swiped her leg under
the other one. He went down with a thud
and lost hold of the blue-spotted egg. As it
flew into the air, Ghost-Spider's hand shot
out. She caught it just in time.

"See!" she said to no one in particular. "Super hero reflexes save the day again!" She bound the second henchman's hands and feet in a web, then turned to leave with the egg. But the sound of enormous flapping wings made her look up. The Vulture was headed right for her! Ghost-Spider braced for impact.

"Squawk!" The rare bird swooped in and bumped the Vulture off his path. The villain slammed into the back of the van and was knocked out cold. Ghost-Spider webbed the van doors shut and headed for the alley.

"Thanks for the help!" she said to the bird. She found her backpack and placed the blue-spotted egg inside. "Don't worry, I'll keep your baby safe. Follow me. I know somewhere that can help you both."

"Squawk!" the bird replied. And they took to the sky.

# Chapter 3:

# *RUFFLED FEATHERS*

"Don't worry, Ghost-Spider," said the counselor at the Animal Care Center. "We'll take good care of your friend." She helped the bird into a birdcage much nicer than the crate from the warehouse.

"Thanks," Ghost-Spider said. She looked at her watch. "Yikes! I'm going to be late. Sorry I have to go, birdie. But you're in good hands here. See you later!" Ghost-Spider was halfway to the door when the mother bird screeched. She pointed her beak at Gwen's backpack.

"I almost forgot!" Ghost-Spider said. "Your egg!" She unzipped her bag and thrust her hand inside. "Here you go," she said as she gave an egg to the counselor. "Take care of this little one, too. Gotta run!"

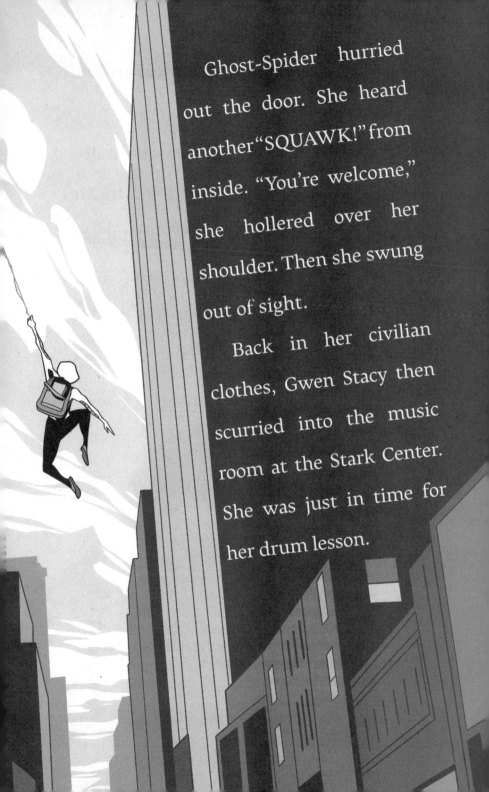

Ghost-Spider hurried out the door. She heard another "SQUAWK!" from inside. "You're welcome," she hollered over her shoulder. Then she swung out of sight.

Back in her civilian clothes, Gwen Stacy then scurried into the music room at the Stark Center. She was just in time for her drum lesson.

"Hey, Gwen," another drummer named Camilla said. "Your backpack's open."

Gwen gasped. "My egg! How could I be so careless?" She slipped her hand inside her bag and pulled out a smooth, uncracked egg. "Phew." Gwen let out a relieved sigh. "I'm supposed to take care of this egg for homework. Looks like I need to pay a bit more attention."

Camilla stared at the egg. "That's a neat assignment," she said. "It's cool that you got such a unique egg."

"Unique?" said Gwen. "But it's just a regular old—" She didn't finish her sentence. Gwen stared at the egg in her hand. It was bigger than she remembered. And a different color. And last time she'd checked, it didn't have blue spots!

*Oh no!* Gwen thought. *I must have left the wrong egg at the Animal Care Center!* She grabbed her backpack, carefully placed the egg back inside, and zipped it up tight. "Camilla," she said, "will you tell the instructor I had to go? Thanks!" She ran off without waiting for a reply.

Back in her super hero suit, Ghost-Spider soared through the air. She spoke to the rare bird's egg nestled inside her backpack. "Sorry for the mix-up," she said. "I'll get you back to your mama in no time. The Animal Care Center is just on the next block."

But as Ghost-Spider turned the corner, she was met with an unwelcome sight. For the second time today, she saw the Vulture! His henchmen were once again loading a birdcage into the back of their van.

"Victory!" the Vulture cried. They drove off with the rare bird . . . and Gwen's homework egg!

# Chapter 4:

# WILD-GOOSE CHASE

Sitting on the curb outside the animal center staring into her open backpack, Ghost-Spider smiled at the blue-spotted egg. "I promise to be way more careful with any eggs in my possession," she said. "But first we have to go on a big chase to get your mama back. So I'm going to make you nice and safe." She spun a thick, cushioning web around the egg. "Don't worry. I've got a plan. Ready to save the day?"

The egg did not object.

Ghost-Spider zipped up her backpack. She secured both straps on her shoulders, then swung to the top of the nearest skyscraper. "Now let's see where that van went." She scanned the streets below until she spotted a police car chasing a white van. What looked like a human-sized bird flew alongside it. "Bingo," Ghost-Spider said. And she dove into the afternoon sky.

"Hey, Vulchy," said Ghost-Spider as she swung up alongside her feathery foe.

"Buzz off," the Vulture snapped. He swiped a metal talon at her. She ducked. It missed.

"Is that any way to treat the hero who has your precious egg?" she asked.

"What are you talking about?" the Vulture demanded. "The egg's in the cage with the bird!"

Ghost-Spider shrugged. "You sure about that?"

The Vulture radioed to his henchmen. "Check the egg," he instructed.

"It's here," one of them replied. "All tiny and shiny and white. Wait a minute. What happened to its blue spots?"

"No!" the Vulture cried.

"Come and get it," Ghost-Spider said as she whipped around the corner and turned onto the next street.

"Follow that spider!" screamed the Vulture. The van drove after her. The police car followed.

"It's a good thing I know this city better than the Vulture and his friends," Ghost-Spider told the blue-spotted egg nestled in her backpack. She turned into another street. The Vulture, van, and police car pursued. "Because if they were paying attention—"

She took a right.

"—they'd realize—"

She took a left.

"—that I'm taking

them back to—"

She took another left.

"—the Animal Care Center."

Ghost-Spider sped over a crosswalk

and down the connecting avenue.

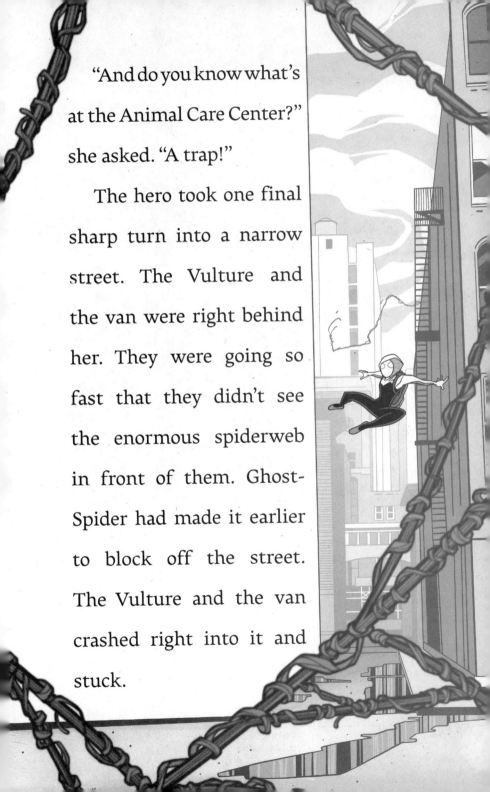

"And do you know what's at the Animal Care Center?" she asked. "A trap!"

The hero took one final sharp turn into a narrow street. The Vulture and the van were right behind her. They were going so fast that they didn't see the enormous spiderweb in front of them. Ghost-Spider had made it earlier to block off the street. The Vulture and the van crashed right into it and stuck.

The police car came to a stop at the other end of the street, relieved the chase had ended. "Now, that's what I call a sticky situation," one of the officers said.

"This is not how this was supposed to go!"

the Vulture cried. The police officers placed

him and his henchmen under arrest.

"Squawk!" a voice came from inside

the van. Ghost-Spider ran to the back and

threw open the doors.

"It's okay," she told the distressed rare bird as she unlatched the cage. "I've got your egg! And I think you have mine. Want to trade?"

"Squawk!" the bird replied.

Carefully, Ghost-Spider pulled the blue-spotted egg from her backpack. The mother bird flapped her wings. Then she stood up from her nest and revealed Gwen's homework egg.

The counselor from the Animal Care Center came running outside. "Let me help," she said. She carefully approached the bird and exchanged the eggs.

The rare bird cuddled her egg. "Coo," the bird said.

"I couldn't agree more," Ghost-Spider replied with a smile. And she gave her own egg the biggest—and gentlest—hug.

# Chapter 5:

# TIME TO NEST

"The bird and her egg will be moved to an aviary sanctuary tonight," said the Animal Care Center counselor.

"You hear that, birdie?" said Ghost-Spider. "You and your baby will have a new home where you'll be free and safe."

"Squawk!" the bird replied.

"I'll visit when your egg hatches," the

hero promised. Then she waved goodbye and slipped into a nearby alley.

Ghost-Spider held her own egg up to her face. "I'm sorry for not taking better care of you, little eggy," she said. "I thought being the strongest and the fastest automatically made me responsible. But taking care of your needs and keeping you safe was what I should have done from the start. I will do a better job with this homework assignment from now on. And not just so I get a good grade. But because I promised to be your protector.

It's the responsible thing to do."

The egg silently agreed.

"What do you say we go back to the Stark Center?" Ghost-Spider asked. "I can play for you." Before the egg could reply, another spider-hero in a black suit with a red spider woven on the front and the back swung onto the scene.

"Sorry to interrupt," said Ghost-Spider's friend Spider-Man. "A little birdie told me the Vulture was in town. So I came to help. But it looks like you already took care of everything." He looked at the egg

in Ghost-Spider's hand. "Also . . . were you talking to an egg?"

"It's a long story," Ghost-Spider said.

"Is it an *eggciting* one?" Spider-Man asked.

Ghost-Spider laughed. "It was pretty *eggcellent.*"

"Hey," said Spider-Man, "want to go patrolling tonight? I hear the Green Goblin's got a new glider. And that can only spell trouble."

Ghost-Spider shook her head. "I'll leave that to you this time," she said. "My egg and I have had enough adventure for one day."

Ghost-Spider webbed a cocoon around her egg. She placed it gently in her backpack. She zipped the bag closed and webbed the zipper extra tight. Then she slipped on the straps.

"Ready, little eggy?" she said. "Let's fly!"

Ghost-Spider and her egg swung gracefully into the night.

# TAKE A STEP BACK

KZZZT!

Shuri threw her hands up in frustration as her kimoyo beads shorted out again. She was the princess of Wakanda and the country's resident super genius, yet she couldn't figure out how to stabilize her latest invention.

Shuri knew exactly how her new

invention *should* work. "I'm almost there" she said to her personal AI assistant. "I just need to turn my kimoyo beads from a simple communication device to something that can not only disrupt the transmission of other tech, but take control of it too."

"Yes, Princess. If anyone can complete the update, it's you," Shuri's AI encouraged.

"Enough with the flattery," she murmured to shush the assistant.

Shuri called her new invention the "remote control," but so far all of her attempts to make it work had ended in failure and the smell of fried electronics. She could get her beads to disrupt transmissions easily, but taking control was proving to be much harder.

Shuri sighed. "The world considers me a genius, but I cannot even figure out how to install a new feature on my own invention."

The princess was rarely startled, but leave it to the Black Panther to make a silent entrance. "Come, now. Do not give up," came her brother's voice from behind. Shuri jumped. Her brother, T'Challa, was not only the king of Wakanda, but also the super hero the Black Panther. While T'Challa was strong and noble, he was not always necessarily right. At least not to Shuri, anyway. She needed to take her mind off her project.